The Tale of Ferdinand Frog

By

Arthur Scott Bailey

THE TALE OF FERDINAND FROG

I

PRETTY AS A PICTURE

There was something about Ferdinand Frog that made everybody smile. It may have been his amazingly wide mouth and his queer, bulging eyes, or perhaps it was his sprightly manner—for one never could tell when Mr. Frog would leap into the air, or turn a somersault backward. Indeed, some of his neighbors claimed that he himself didn't know what he was going to do next—he was so jumpy.

Anyhow, all the wild folk in Pleasant Valley agreed that Ferdinand Frog was an agreeable person to have around. No matter what happened, he was always cheerful. Nobody ever heard of his losing his temper, though to be sure he was sometimes the means of other peoples losing theirs. But let a body be as angry as he pleased with Mr. Frog, Mr. Frog would continue to smile and smirk.

Of course, such extreme cheerfulness often made angry folk only the more furious, especially when the whole trouble was Ferdinand Frog's own fault. But it made no difference to him what blunder he had made. He was always ready to make another—and smile at the same time.

Really, he was so good-natured that nobody could feel peevish towards him for long. In fact, he was a great favorite—especially among the ladies. Whenever he met one of them—it might be the youngest of the Rabbit sisters, or old Aunt Polly Woodchuck—he never failed to make the lowest of bows, smile the broadest of smiles, and inquire after her health.

That was Ferdinand Frog—known far and wide for his elegant manners. Every young lady declared that he wore exquisite clothes, too; and many of them secretly thought him quite good-looking.

But people as old as Aunt Polly Woodchuck seldom take heed of what a person wears. As for Mr. Frog's looks, since Aunt Polly believed that "handsome is as handsome does," she admitted that Ferdinand Frog was—as she put it—"purty as a picter."

When Ferdinand Frog heard that, he was so delighted that he hurried straight home and put on his best suit. And then he spent most of a whole afternoon smiling at his reflection in the surface of the Beaver pond, where he was living at the time.

So it is easy to see that Ferdinand Frog was a vain and silly fellow. He was even foolish enough to repeat Aunt Polly's remark to everybody he chanced to meet that night, and the following day as well.

There was no one who could help grinning at Ferdinand Frog's news—he looked so comical. And old Mr. Crow, who was noted for his rudeness, even burst out with a hoarse haw-haw.

"You're pretty as a picture, eh?" he chuckled. "I suppose Aunt Polly means that you're as pretty as one of the pictures that the circus men have pasted on Farmer Green's barn. . . . I believe——" he added, as he stared at Ferdinand Frog——"I believe I know which one Aunt Polly means."

"Is that so?" cried Mr. Frog, swelling himself up—through pride—until it seemed that he must burst. "Oh, which picture is it?"

"It's the one in the upper left-hand corner," old Mr. Crow informed him solemnly. "And if you haven't yet seen it, you should take a good look at it soon."

"I will!" Ferdinand Frog declared. "I'll visit Farmer Green's place this very night!"

And he opened his mouth and smiled so widely that old Mr. Crow couldn't help shuddering—though he knew well enough that Ferdinand Frog could never swallow anyone as big as he was.

II
THE DANGERS OF TRAVEL

It was a long way to Farmer Green's from the Beaver pond where Ferdinand Frog made his home. But he felt that he simply must see that picture which Mr. Crow said looked like him. So he started out just before sunset.

One thing, at least, about his journey pleased him: he could make the trip by water—and he certainly did hate travelling on land.

Luckily the stream that trickled its way below the Beaver dam led straight to Swift River. And everybody who knew anything was aware that Swift River ran right under the bridge not far from the farmhouse.

So Mr. Frog leaped spryly into the brook and struck out downstream.

He was a famous swimmer, having been used to the water from the time he was a tadpole. And now he swam so fast, with the help of the current, that he reached the river by the time the moon was up.

As he looked up at the sky Ferdinand Frog was both glad and sorry that there was a moon that night. The moon would be a good thing, provided he reached the end of his journey, for it would give him a fine clear view of the picture on the barn, which he so much wanted to see. On the other hand, he would have preferred a dark night for a swim in Swift River. There were fish there—pickerel—which would rather swallow him than not. And he knew that they were sure to be feeding by the light of the moon.

If Mr. Frog hadn't always looked on the bright side of life no doubt he would have waited a week or two, until there was no moon at all. But he remarked to himself with a grin, as he hurried along, that he had never yet seen the pickerel that was quick enough to catch him, and furthermore, he never expected to.

But those words were hardly out of Ferdinand Frog's mouth when he turned and made for the bank as fast as he could go. He had caught sight of a dark, long-nosed fish lying among some weeds. And he decided suddenly that he would finish his journey by land.

"It would be a shame——" he told himself, as he flopped up the steep bank——"it would be a shame for so handsome a person as I am to be eaten by a fish."

"But you wouldn't object to a bird, would you?" said a voice right in Ferdinand Frog's ear—or so it seemed to him.

He made no answer—not even stopping to bow, or say good evening—but turned a somersault backward and hid himself under the overhanging bank.

It was Solomon Owl who had spoken to him. There was no mistaking the loud, mocking laughter that followed Mr. Frog's hasty retreat.

"Solomon Owl is a great joker," Mr. Frog murmured with a smile. "He was only teasing me. . . . Still, he might be a bit hungry. So I'll stay here out of harm's way for a while, for it would be a shame for so handsome a person as I am to be eaten by an old, rascally bird like Solomon Owl."

One can judge, just by that remark, that Ferdinand Frog was not quite so polite as his neighbors supposed—when there was no one to hear what he said.

III
MR. FROG'S DOUBLE

Mr. Frog waited until it was broad daylight before he left his hiding place beneath the bank of the river. He knew that by that time Solomon Owl must have gone home to his hemlock tree to get his rest. So Ferdinand Frog felt quite safe again.

Having made up his mind that he would finish his journey to Farmer Green's place by land, he started briskly across the cornfield, travelling in a straight line between two rows of young corn.

He had not gone far before a hoarse voice called to him. But this time he was not alarmed.

It was only old Mr. Crow, who seemed greatly pleased to see him.

"Hullo, young fellow!" said Mr. Crow. "If you're on your way to the barn to look at that picture, I'll fly over there myself, because I'd like to see it again."

"Aren't you afraid of meeting Farmer Green?" Ferdinand Frog asked him.

"Afraid?" Mr. Crow snorted. "Certainly not! We're the best of friends. He set up this straw man here, just to keep me company. . . . Besides," he went on, "at this time o' day Farmer Green is inside the barn, milking the cows. And we'll be outside it, looking at the circus pictures."

"We can call to him, if you want to say good morning to him," Ferdinand Frog suggested cheerfully.

"Oh, no!" his companion said quickly. "I wouldn't want to do that—he's so busy."

Ferdinand Frog smiled. And for some reason old Mr. Crow seemed displeased.

"What's the joke?" he inquired in a surly tone. "Something seems to amuse you. Why are you grinning?"

"It's just a habit I have," Ferdinand Frog explained.

"I'd try to break myself of that habit, if I were you," Mr. Crow advised him. "Some day it will get you into trouble, for you're likely to grin when you oughtn't to. There's a wrong time and a right time for everything, you know."

"Just as there is for planting corn," Mr. Frog chimed in.

"Exactly!" Mr. Crow returned.

"And for eating it!" Mr. Frog added.

But old Mr. Crow only said hastily that he would be at the barn by the time Ferdinand reached it. And without another word he flapped himself away across the field.

"He's a queer one," said Ferdinand Frog to himself. "It seems as if a person couldn't please him, no matter how much a person tried." Then he untied his necktie, and tied it again, because he thought one end of the bow was longer than the other; and that was something he couldn't endure.

Then he resumed his jumping. And after exactly one hundred and thirty-two jumps he reached a corner of Farmer Green's great barn, where he found old Mr. Crow waiting for him.

"Still smiling, I see," the old gentleman observed gruffly. "Maybe you'll laugh out of the other corner of your mouth after you've seen the pretty picture that you look like."

"I hope so! Where is it?" Ferdinand Frog asked him eagerly. "Show me the pretty one!"

"Come with me!" said old Mr. Crow. And he led the way around the barn, stopping before the side that faced the road.

"There!" he cried. "It's in the upper left-hand corner, just as I told you." And he chuckled as loud as he dared—with Farmer Green inside the building, milking the cows.

As Ferdinand Frog gazed upward a shadow of disappointment came over his face. And for once he did not smile.

"Do I look like that?" he faltered.

"You certainly do," old Mr. Crow assured him. "See those eyes—don't they bulge just like yours? And look at that mouth! It's fully as wide as yours—and maybe a trifle wider!"

"The face does look a bit like mine, I'll admit," Ferdinand Frog muttered. "But no one could ever mistake one of us for the other. . . . What's the name of this creature?"

"It's called the hippopotamus," old Mr. Crow replied. "I heard Johnnie Green say so. And he ought to know, if anyone does."

IV
MR. CROW LOSES SOMETHING

The picture of the hippopotamus on Farmer Green's barn did not please Ferdinand Frog. But in a few moments he began to smile again.

"You've made a mistake," he told old Mr. Crow with a snicker. "When Aunt Polly Woodchuck said I was as pretty as a picture she never could have had this one in mind."

"Why not?" Mr. Crow inquired. "The eyes and the mouth——"

"Yes! Yes—I know!" Ferdinand interrupted. "But this creature has a tail! And tails are terribly out of fashion. I haven't worn one since I was a tadpole."

That was enough for old Mr. Crow. He had a tail——or tail feathers, at least. And he at once flew into a terrible rage.

"You've insulted me!" he shouted.

Ferdinand Frog knew then that he had blundered. So he hastened to mend matters.

"There, there!" he said in a soothing tone. "Having a tail is not so bad, after all; for you can always cut it off, if you want to be in style." And he was surprised to find that his remark only made Mr. Crow angrier than ever.

"Cut off my tail, indeed!" the old gentleman snorted. "I'd be a pretty sight, if I did. Why, I wouldn't part with a single tail-feather, on any account." He continued to scold Ferdinand Frog at the top of his lungs, telling him that he was a silly fellow, and that nobody—unless it was a few foolish young creatures—thought he was the least bit handsome.

Now, old Mr. Crow was in such a temper that he forgot that Farmer Green was inside the barn. And he made so much noise that Farmer Green heard him and peeped around the corner of the barn to see what was going on.

A moment later the old shot-gun went off with a terrific roar. Ferdinand Frog saw Mr. Crow spring up and go tearing off towards the woods. And a long, black tail-feather floated slowly down out of the air and settled on the ground near the place where Mr. Crow had been standing.

After shaking his fist in Mr. Crow's direction, Farmer Green disappeared.

"That's a pity," Mr. Frog thought. "Mr. Crow has parted with one of his tail-feathers. And I must find him as soon as I can and tell him how sorry I am."

Then Mr. Frog turned to look at the other pictures, which covered the whole side of the big barn. He beheld many strange creatures—some with necks of enormous length, some with humps on their backs, and all of them of amazing colors.

But whether they were ringed, streaked or striped, not one of them was—in Mr. Frog's opinion—one-half as beautiful as the hippopotamus.

"Even he——" Mr. Frog decided——"even he couldn't be called half as handsome as I am. For once old Mr. Crow certainly was mistaken."

And he began to laugh. And while he was laughing, Farmer Green came out of the barn with a pail of milk in each hand.

Then Ferdinand Frog had a happy thought. Why not ask Farmer Green to shoot off the tail of the hippopotamus? The loss of that ugly tail would improve the creature's looks, and make him appear still more like Mr. Frog himself.

At least, that was Mr. Frog's own opinion.

And he called to Farmer Green and suggested to him that he step out behind the barn and take a shot at the tail of the hippopotamus.

"Try your luck!" Mr. Frog coaxed. "It's plain to see that you need practice, or you'd have made Mr. Crow part with all his tail-feathers, instead of only one." And he laughed harder than ever.

But Farmer Green paid little heed to Ferdinand Frog's wheedling, although he did smile and say:

"I declare, I believe that bull frog's jeering at me because I missed the old crow!"

V
MR. FROG'S SECRET SORROW

Ferdinand Frog always looked so cheerful that no one ever suspected that he had a secret sorrow. But it is true, nevertheless, that something troubled him, though he took great pains not to let a single one of his neighbors know that anything grieved him.

His trouble was simply this: he had never been invited to attend the singing-parties which the Frog family held almost every evening in Cedar Swamp.

Now, Ferdinand Frog loved to sing at night.

Indeed, he liked nothing better than to go to the lake not far from the Beaver dam and practice his songs among the lily pads near the shore. He had a deep, powerful bass voice, which one could hear a mile or more across the water on a still evening.

Often he dressed himself with the greatest care and went to the lake alone, where he stayed half the night and sang so loudly that a good many of the wild folk who lived in the neighborhood thought him a great nuisance. Not caring for music, they objected to being forced to listen to Ferdinand Frog's favorite songs.

"Why don't you go over to Cedar Swamp, if you want to make a noise?" one of the Beaver family who was known as Tired Tim asked Mr. Frog one evening. "You have come here for nine nights running; and your racket has upset me so that I haven't done a stroke of work in all this time."

Mr. Frog had puffed himself up and had just opened his mouth to begin a new song. But upon being spoken to so rudely he closed his mouth quickly and swallowed several times. For just a second or two he was speechless, he was so surprised. And then presently he began to giggle.

"I believe you," he said. "I believe that you haven't done a stroke of work for ninety nights." He knew—as did everybody else—that Tired Tim was the laziest person for miles around.

"I said nine—not ninety," Tired Tim corrected him.

"Oh! My mistake!" Mr. Frog replied.

"You haven't answered my question," Tired Tim reminded him with a wide yawn. "I asked you why you didn't attend the singing-parties over in Cedar Swamp. You could croak your head off there and no one would stop you."

But Mr. Frog shook his head. And at the same time, he sighed.

"No!" he said. "I'd rather sing here on the border of the lake. The trouble is, I sing too well for those fellows over in Cedar Swamp."

"Why don't you join them and teach them how to sing, if you know so much about it?" Tired Tim persisted.

"Oh, I've no time for that," Ferdinand Frog answered.

And then it was his companion's turn to snicker.

"You appear to have plenty of time to waste here," he observed. "It's my opinion that there's just one reason why you don't go to the Cedar Swamp singing parties."

"What's that?" Mr. Frog inquired with a slight trace of uneasiness.

"They haven't invited you."

"How did you guess that?" Ferdinand Frog asked him.

He wished, the next moment, that he had not put that question to Tired Tim. For he saw at once that he had given his sad secret away.

VI

TIRED TIM DOES A FAVOR

In spite of all Ferdinand Frog's teasing, Tired Tim Beaver refused to explain how he happened to know Mr. Frog's secret.

To tell the truth, he had guessed the reason why Mr. Frog did not attend the Cedar Swamp singing-parties. But he hoped that Ferdinand Frog would think that some of the musical Frog family had been talking to him. And he even hinted to Mr. Frog that maybe it would be possible to get him an invitation to the singing-parties.

"Do you think you could do that?" Ferdinand Frog asked him with, great eagerness.

"I might be able to; but it wouldn't be an easy matter," Tired Tim replied. "And I'd expect you to do something for me, if I went to so much trouble on your account."

"I'll do anything for you, in return for an invitation to the Cedar Swamp singing-parties," Ferdinand Frog declared.

"Very well!" Tired Tim told him. "I'll go right over to the swamp now. And when I tell 'em a few things, I know they'll want you to join 'em."

Ferdinand Frog felt so gay that he stood on his head and waved his feet in the air.

"Let's meet here to-morrow night," he suggested.

But Tired Tim objected to that plan.

"You would be hanging about this place—and singing—for four-and-twenty hours," he grumbled. "It will be a great deal better if we meet on the edge of the swamp."

"Just as you wish!" Ferdinand Frog exclaimed. "And since you're going to Cedar Swamp, I'll hop along with you, to keep you company."

"You forget——" said Tired Tim Beaver——"you forget that you haven't been invited yet."

"Have you?" Mr. Frog inquired.

"Certainly!" said Tired Tim. And grinning over his shoulder, he swam away.

Mr. Frog watched his friend from the shore.

"He can't fool me," he muttered. "Tired Tim invited himself. And I've been stupid not to do likewise."

On the following night Ferdinand Frog went to the edge of Cedar Swamp, where he waited somewhat impatiently on a log until Tired Tim Beaver joined him.

"Well!" Mr. Frog cried. "I'm glad to see you and I hope you've brought my invitation."

But Tired Tim wouldn't say yes or no.

"If I succeed in getting you into the Cedar Swamp singing-parties will you promise me that you won't sing any more around the lake, or near our pond, either?" he demanded.

Ferdinand Frog gave his solemn promise.

"Very well, then!" Tired Tim said. "Go along over to the swamp. They're expecting you."

When he heard the good news Ferdinand Frog was so delighted that he leaped into the air and kicked his heels together.

And then forgetting his solemn promise, he began to bellow at the top of his voice:

"To Cedar Swamp I'll haste away;

Though first I'll sing a song.

My voice I must not waste to-day,

So I'll not keep you long.

I simply want to let you know

I'm much obliged, before I go."

"Don't mention it!" said Tired Tim.

"Don't interrupt me, please!" said Ferdinand Frog. "I haven't finished thanking you yet. That's only the first verse."

"How many more are there?" Tired Tim inquired with a yawn.

"Ninety-nine!" Mr. Frog answered. And he was somewhat surprised—and puzzled—when Tired Tim left him suddenly and plunged into the underbrush.

VII

THE SINGING-PARTY

Ferdinand Frog lost no time, after Tired Tim left him. He jumped into the swamp and made straight towards the very middle of it, whence he could already hear the chorus of the numerous Frog family; for the singing-party had begun.

Mr. Frog made all haste, not wishing to miss any more of the fun. Now swimming, now leaping from one hummock to another—or sometimes to an old stump—he quickly reached the place where the Frog family were enjoying themselves.

"Here he is!" several of the singers exclaimed as soon as Ferdinand Frog's head popped out of the water, in their midst.

He saw at once that they had been expecting him; and he smiled and bowed—and waited for the company to stop singing and give him a warm greeting with their cold, damp hands. But except for those first few words, no one paid the slightest attention to the newcomer.

In fact, nobody even took the trouble to nod to Ferdinand Frog—much less to shake hands with him and tell him that he was welcome.

Meanwhile one song followed another with hardly a pause between them. And Mr. Frog found that he did not know the words of even one.

He was so impatient that at last he climbed upon an old fallen tree-trunk, which stuck out of the greenish-black water, and began to roar his favorite song, while he beat time for the other singers. The name of that song was "A Frog on a Log in a Bog"; and Ferdinand Frog thought that he couldn't have chosen another so fitting.

But the rest of the singing-party had other ideas. They turned about and scowled at Mr. Frog as if he had done something most unpleasant.

"Stop! Stop!" several of them cried. And an important-looking fellow near him shouted, "Don't sing that, for pity's sake!"

"Why not?" Ferdinand Frog faltered. "What's the matter with my song? It's my special favorite, which I sing at least fifty times each night, regularly."

"It's old stuff," the other told him with a sneer. "We haven't sung that for a year, at least."

Ferdinand Frog did not try to argue with him. But as soon as he saw another chance he began a different ditty.

Then a loud groan arose. And somebody stopped him again. And Mr. Frog soon learned that they hadn't sung that one for a year and a half.

Though he tried again and again, he had no better luck. But he kept smiling bravely. And finally he asked the company in a loud voice if he "wasn't going to have a chance."

"Certainly!" a number of the singers assured him. "Your chance is coming later. We shan't forget you."

And that made Ferdinand Frog feel better. He told himself that he could wait patiently for a time—if it wasn't too long.

VIII

THE MISSING SUPPER

Ferdinand Frog had begun to feel uneasy again. He was afraid that the singers had forgotten their promise to him. But at last they suddenly started a rousing song which made him take heart again.

They roared out the chorus in a joyful way which left no doubt in his mind that his chance was at hand:

"Now that the concert is ended

We'll sit at the banquet and feast.

Now that the singing's suspended

We'll dine till it's gray in the east."

Mr. Frog only hoped that the company did not expect him to sing to them all the time while they were banqueting.

"They needn't think—" he murmured under his breath—"they needn't think I don't like good things to eat as well as they do." But he let no one see that he was worried. That was Ferdinand Frog's way: almost always he managed to smile, no matter how things went.

When the last echoes of the song had died away a great hubbub arose. Everybody crowded around Mr. Frog. And there were cries of "Now! Now!"

He thought, of course, that they wanted to hear him sing. So he started once more to sing his favorite song. But they stopped him quickly.

"We've finished the songs for to-night," they told him. "We're ready for the supper now. . . . Where is it?"

"Supper?" Mr. Frog faltered, as his jaw dropped. "What supper?"

"The supper you're going to give us!" the whole company shouted. "You know—don't you?—that we have just made a rule for new members: they're to furnish a banquet."

Ferdinand Frog's eyes seemed to bulge further out of his head than ever.

"I—I never heard of this before!" he stammered.

"Didn't Tired Tim tell you about our new rule?" somebody inquired. "It was his own idea."

"He never said a word to me about it!" Ferdinand Frog declared with a loud laugh. "And I can't give you a supper, for I haven't one ready."

"Then we'll postpone it until to-morrow night," the company told him hopefully.

"What does your rule say?" Ferdinand Frog rolled his eyes as he put the question to them.

"It says that the banquet must take place the first night the new member is present," a fat gentleman replied.

"Then I can't give you any food to-morrow night," Mr. Frog informed them, "because it would be against the rule."

"Then you can't be a member!" a hundred voices croaked.

"I am one now," Ferdinand Frog replied happily. "And what's more, I don't see how you can keep me out of your singing-parties."

There was silence for a time.

"We've been sold," some one said at last. "We've no rule to prevent this fellow from coming here. And the worst of it is, as everybody knows, his voice is so loud it will spoil all our songs."

Oddly enough, the speaker was the very one who had always objected to inviting Ferdinand Frog to join the singing parties. His own voice had always been the loudest in the whole company. And naturally he did not want anybody with a louder one to come and drown his best notes.

But now he couldn't help himself. And thereafter when the singers met in Cedar Swamp he always turned greener in the face than ever and looked as if he were about to burst, when Ferdinand Frog opened his mouth its widest and let his voice rumble forth into the night.

IX

THE MYSTERIOUS STRANGER

When Ferdinand Frog first came to the Beaver pond to live no one knew anything about him.

He appeared suddenly—no one knew whence—and at once made himself very much at home. It was no time at all before he could call every one of the big Beaver family by name. And he acted exactly as if the pond belonged to him, instead of to the Beavers, whose great-grandfathers had dammed the stream many years before.

But the newcomer was so polite that nobody cared to send him away. At the same time, people couldn't help wondering who the stranger was and where he had come from and what his plans for the future were. Whenever two or three Beavers stopped working long enough to enjoy a pleasant chat, they were sure to talk of the mysterious Mr. Frog and tell one another what they thought of him. Many were the tales told about the nimble fellow.

Some said that he had moved all the way from Farmer Green's duck pond, because Johnnie Green had tried to catch him; while others declared that Ferdinand Frog was a famous singer, who had come to that quiet spot in order to rest his voice, which had become harsh from too much use. Indeed, there were so many stories about the stranger that it was hard to know which to believe—especially after old Mr. Crow informed Brownie Beaver that in his opinion Ferdinand Frog was a slippery fellow. "I shouldn't be surprised——" Mr. Crow had said with a wise wag of his head——"I shouldn't be surprised if his real name was Ferdinand Fraud."

Anyhow, there was one thing that almost all the Beaver colony agreed upon. They were of one opinion as to Mr. Frog's clothes, which they thought must be very fashionable, because they were like no others that had ever been seen before in those parts.

There was one young gentleman, however—the beau of the village—who disputed everybody, saying that he believed that Ferdinand Frog must be wearing old clothes that were many years behind the times.

Now, there was one lazy Beaver known as Tired Tim who had nothing better to do than to go straight to Mr. Frog and repeat what he heard.

To Tired Tim's surprise—for he had expected Mr. Frog to lose his temper—to his surprise that gentleman appeared much amused by the bit of gossip. He shook with silent laughter for a time, quite as if he were saving his voice to use that evening. And then he said:

"So your young friend thinks I'm not in style, eh? . . . Well, I'll tell you something: he's right, in a way. And in another way he isn't. The reason why I'm not in style is because I always aim to keep five years ahead of everybody else.

"Five years from now and your neighbors will all be wearing clothes like mine."

"Can't we ever catch up with you?" Tired Tim asked him.

"There's only one way you can do that," was Mr. Frog's mysterious answer.

And he would say no more.

X
CATCHING UP WITH MR. FROG

Tired Tim Beaver asked Mr. Frog point-blank how a person might catch up with him in the matter of clothes.

"If you manage to dress in a style that's five years ahead of the times, I should like to know the way to be just as fashionable," Tired Tim said.

But he got no help—then—from Mr. Frog. All Ferdinand Frog would say was that he'd be glad to oblige a friend, but he couldn't—and wouldn't—be hurried.

And though the unhappy, eager Tim teased and begged him to tell his secret, Mr. Frog only smiled the more cheerfully and said nothing.

It was maddening—for Tired Tim—though Mr. Frog seemed to be enjoying himself hugely. And the result was that Tired Tim Beaver returned to the village in the pond in a terrible state of mind. Since he told everyone else what he had learned about Ferdinand Frog and his clothes, it was only a short time before the whole Beaver family was so stirred up that they couldn't do a stroke of work. Ferdinand Frog was in everybody's mouth, so to speak. And at last old Grandaddy Beaver hit upon a plan.

"Why don't you get somebody to make you a suit exactly like Mr. Frog's?" he asked Tired Tim.

So Tired Tim took Grandaddy's advice. That very night he disappeared, to swagger back in a few days in a costume that made him appear almost like Mr. Frog's twin brother—if one didn't look at his face. And there were some among the villagers who even declared that Tired Tim's mouth seemed wider than it had been, and more like Mr. Frog's.

When they asked Tired Tim if his tailor hadn't stretched his mouth for him he replied no, that he had been smiling a good deal for a day or two, and perhaps that was what made his mouth look different.

Well, the whole Beaver village was delighted with Tired Tim's new suit.

"Wait till Mr. Frog sees you!" people cried. "He'll be so surprised!"

And somebody swam away in great haste to find Mr. Frog and ask him to come to the lower end of the pond, where all the houses were. But when Ferdinand Frog arrived, everybody was disappointed, and especially Tired Tim, who had felt very proud in his gorgeous new clothes. For he saw at once that Mr. Frog was arrayed from head to foot in an entirely new outfit. He looked almost like a rainbow, so brilliant were the colors of his costume.

At the same time Tired Tim put on as brave a front as he could. And drawing near to Mr. Frog, he said:

"What do you think of my new suit?"

Ferdinand Frog looked at him as if he hadn't noticed him before.

"Your suit's all right," he replied, "for one who isn't particular. But it's not far enough ahead of the times for me. . . . I'd hate to be caught wearing it."

It was a bitter blow for Tired Tim Beaver. In fact, he felt more tired than ever; and he sank to the bottom of the pond to rest, where his friends couldn't see him.

As for the other members of the Beaver family, they all went home with a great longing inside them. There wasn't a single one of them that wasn't eager to wear clothes exactly as far ahead of the times as were those of the elegant stranger, Ferdinand Frog.

XI

FERDINAND FROG IS IN NO HURRY

Although everybody in the Beaver village looked worried, Mr. Frog seemed to be all the more cheerful. He knew well enough that there was hardly one Beaver in the pond that didn't wish and long for clothes which were, like Mr. Frog's, five years ahead of the times.

As day after day passed, not only were the Beavers unable to do a single stroke of work; they were so upset that they could scarcely eat or sleep. And at last the older villagers, such as Grandaddy Beaver, began to see that something would have to be done. There was the dam, which needed mending; and there was the winter's food, which had to be gathered.

So Grandaddy Beaver went to Ferdinand Frog one day and told him that he simply must come to the rescue of the pond folk, and tell them how they might have clothes as far ahead of the times as were his own.

"Why?" Mr. Frog inquired. "What's the trouble?"

"They can't work," Grandaddy Beaver told him. "And there's the dam to be fixed, and tree-tops to be cut and stored for food, because winter's a-coming, and there's no way we can stop it."

"I'll tell you what you and your people can do," Ferdinand Frog replied. "Just bury yourselves in the mud during the winter, as I do, and you'd have no use for a dam, nor for food, either."

But Grandaddy Beaver explained that though such a plan might suit a Frog exceedingly well, for a Beaver it would never do at all.

"You have got us into this scrape," he told Mr. Frog, "so it's only fair that you should help us out of it."

Ferdinand Frog then did a number of things, all of which were intended to let Grandaddy Beaver see that what he asked couldn't be done. Mr. Frog held up his hands with the palms out and rolled his eyes; he shut his great mouth together as if he did not intend to say another word. He looked so determined that Grandaddy Beaver's heart sank.

And then—when Grandaddy Beaver had almost given up all hope—then Mr. Frog said suddenly:

"I'll consent to help you, because I see that it's my duty."

"Good!" Grandaddy Beaver cried. "I told people that I knew you'd come to our rescue, for you have such a kind face! . . .

"And now, tell me!" he bade Ferdinand Frog with great eagerness, while he held a hand behind one of his ears, in order to hear more clearly.

But Mr. Frog was not ready to give away his secret.

He winked at Grandaddy Beaver, and poked his fingers into the old gentleman's ribs.

"Not so fast, my lad!" said Mr. Frog, who was certainly many years younger than Grandaddy Beaver. "I'm not prepared to explain everything to you just yet.

"You come to the big rock on the other side of the pond as soon as it's dark to-night; and bring with you everybody who wants to know how to get clothes like mine.

"Now, do exactly as I say," Mr. Frog cautioned Grandaddy, "and everything will be made easy."

XII

A BAD BLUNDER

When it was almost dark Grandaddy Beaver swam across the pond to the big rock, where Ferdinand Frog had told him to come.

And trooping after Daddy was almost everybody in the village. Not counting the women and children, there were eleven of them. They climbed upon the rock, looking for Mr. Frog. But he was nowhere in sight.

"He'll be here in a minute or two, probably," Grandaddy Beaver said hopefully, for all he looked a bit anxious.

Then somebody spied a neat building near-by, which not one of them had noticed before.

"What's this strange house?" people asked one another. "Is this where Mr. Frog lives?"

But nobody seemed to know the answer to that question.

"It can't be a shop," Grandaddy decided, "for there's no sign on it. And nobody would have a shop without a sign."

Now, the door of the little building was shut and fastened. And the window-shades were pulled carefully down. It certainly looked as if nobody was at home.

But suddenly there came a sound that made the Beaver family jump. It came from the house—there was no doubt of that.

In fact it came right through the keyhole; and it was like nothing in the world but a sneeze.

A number of people were all ready to jump into the water and swim away, they were so startled.

And then a snicker followed the sneeze. And by that time Grandaddy Beaver and his friends guessed who was inside the building. It was

Ferdinand Frog; and he had been watching his callers all the time, through the keyhole, and listening to everything that they said.

A few felt slightly uneasy, as they tried to remember exactly what remarks they had made about Mr. Frog himself.

"Come out!" they all cried, as soon as they had recovered from their surprise. "We want to see you!" And they formed a half-circle in the dooryard.

Presently the door swung out, as if somebody had pushed it open. And there, on the inside of the open door, which was flung back against the outside of the building, they all saw a sign, which said:

MR. FERDINAND FROG

People began exclaiming that that was just like Ferdinand Frog—who was an odd fellow—to have his sign painted on the inside of his door instead of on the outside.

"It'll be all the style five years from now," he retorted.

So that was Mr. Frog's secret! He was a tailor himself! And there he was, ready to make clothes for all of them!

It was almost too good to be true. But there he stood in the doorway, with a tape around his neck, smiling and bowing.

"You'd better form in line!" he suggested. "You can come in through the front door. I'll measure you. And you can pass out the back way. . . . Don't crowd, please!"

Now, that was just where Mr. Frog made a great blunder. But he didn't find it out till it was too late.

XIII

A SIXTY-INCH MEAL

Mr. Frog's scheme of measuring the Beaver family for new suits had just one drawback; the Beaver family liked it too well. So pleased were they over the prospect of having "unfashionable" clothes like Mr. Frog's at last that all of them wanted to be measured not once but several times. And each and every one, as soon as Mr. Frog had taken his measurements, went out through the back door and slipped around the little building, to wait again at the foot of the line.

Now, Mr. Frog was a spry worker. He passed his tape around his customers and jotted down figures on flat, black stones as fast as he could make his fingers fly. And if it hadn't been for just one thing Ferdinand Frog would have been quite happy. But beginning with his first customer, he was somewhat troubled; for in the whole company he found not one who had brought his pocket-book with him.

"What's the matter?" he asked Grandaddy Beaver, when the old gentleman's turn came. "Didn't you tell 'em what I said about pocket-books?"

"I certainly did!" Grandaddy replied. "I told them to be sure to leave their pocket-books at home."

Mr. Frog gulped once or twice, as if he were swallowing something unpleasant. And he looked most surprised.

"Why, that's exactly wrong!" he cried.

"Is that so?" Grandaddy Beaver quavered. "Then I must have made a mistake. You know I'm a leetle hard of hearing."

"Never mind!" Ferdinand Frog answered, for he always took his troubles lightly. "Bring 'em when you come to have your clothes fitted and it'll be all right."

So he worked on. But by and by he began to grow uneasy again. And now and then he paused and went to the window, where he peered somewhat anxiously at the Beavers who waited before his door in a long line.

"It's queer!" Mr. Frog exclaimed aloud at last. "Here I've been measuring 'em for an hour and a half; and there's just as many of 'em left. . . . I'll have to stop soon," he continued, "for I'm going to a singing-party to-night. And I don't want to be late."

His customers, however, wouldn't hear of his leaving. The moment Mr. Frog's remarks passed down the line, the Beaver family began to jostle and push one another. They crowded inside the tailor's shop.

And to get rid of them, Mr. Frog worked faster than ever. So great was his haste that he measured everybody wrong; whereas before he had measured them correctly, while merely scratching wrong figures upon the stones.

And finally he stopped suddenly. As Grandaddy Beaver stepped forward to be measured for the fourth time it dawned upon Mr. Frog that he had measured him several times already.

But Ferdinand Frog said nothing at all.

Holding one end of his tape in his mouth, he passed the other end around Grandaddy's plump body.

All at once a cry of dismay came from the customers who were looking on while they waited.

"He's swallowing the tape!" they cried, pointing to Mr. Frog.

It was true. Beneath their horrified gaze the tape-measure disappeared little by little inside Mr. Frog's mouth. And before any of them could come to his senses and seize the end of the yellow strip, it had vanished from view completely.

Of course they saw that the tailor could work no longer that evening. So they filed sadly out of the shop.

"How did it happen?" they asked Mr. Frog, who was already locking his door.

"The tape stuck to my tongue," he explained. "Everything does, you know. But it doesn't matter, because I was hungry. And now I feel better."

So Mr. Frog reached the singing-party in time, after all.

XIV

AN UNPLEASANT MIX-UP

For a long time after he took the measurements of the Beaver family Mr. Frog kept carefully out of sight. Though several of the Beavers visited his shop every day, they always found the door locked and the shades drawn. But from various odd sounds—such as giggles and titters and snickers—which they heard by listening at the keyhole, they knew that the tailor was inside.

To all their knocks and calls, however, Mr. Frog made no other response. He was working busily, and he did not want to be interrupted.

At last, to the delight of everybody, a notice appeared one evening upon Mr. Frog's door, which said:

TO-MORROW WILL BE

FITTING-DAY

Well, never was such excitement known in the Beaver family—unless it was when the great freshet came, and almost washed away the dam. And it was lucky there was no freshet upon Mr. Frog's fitting-day, for there would have been no one except the women and children to do any work. Some of the young dandies even spent the night right in front of Mr. Frog's tailor's shop, in order to be among the first to try on their new clothes, which were to be five years ahead of the times.

When Mr. Frog opened his door bright and early the following morning he had to beg his eager customers to keep order.

"There's a suit here for everybody," he announced. "But if you crowd into my shop I may get the garments mixed. And that would be terrible."

So the Beaver gentlemen were as quiet and orderly as they could be. But as for Mr. Frog himself, he jumped around as if he were standing in a hot frying-pan. He hustled his customers into their suits in no time, assuring each one that his garments fitted him perfectly, and asking him please to step out through the back door and wait.

By the time the last Beaver had on his new clothes, and Mr. Frog followed him into the back-yard, the tailor found that there was a frightful uproar outside. There wasn't one of the Beavers who didn't claim that there was something wrong about his new clothes. But whether sleeves, trousers or coat-tails were too short or too long, or whether they were too loose or too tight, Mr. Frog declared that they were exactly as they should be, because they were bound to be in style in five years' time, and nobody — so he said — could prove otherwise.

Of course, the Beaver family was far from satisfied. Though they had what they had been wishing for, they couldn't help thinking that they looked very queer — as, indeed, they did.

But Ferdinand Frog told the crowd that it was only because they weren't used to being dressed in that fashion. He said he certainly was pleased with their appearance and that he had never seen any company that looked the least bit like them.

There was one Beaver, however, who shouted angrily that he knew his suit wasn't fashionable and that he wouldn't accept it.

XV
EVERYONE IS HAPPY

Mr. Frog led the angry Beaver around to the front of his shop, while the others followed, and pointed to his sign.

"There!" he said. "Don't you see that I claim to be an unfashionable tailor? You'll have to keep that suit, and pay me for it, too. And so will everybody else."

But the whole Beaver family cried out that they objected. "No one ever pays his tailor," they told Mr. Frog. "It's not the fashionable thing to do."

Even then Ferdinand Frog continued to smile at them. He was such an agreeable chap!

"I know it's not fashionable now," he admitted, "but it will be five years from now. And since it's my way to collect on delivery, I'll thank you to step up one at a time and pay me. . . . And please don't crowd!" he added.

There was really no need of that last warning, because nobody made a move.

Mr. Frog, however, was not dismayed. He leaped suddenly into the air and alighted directly in front of a Beaver known among his friends as Stingy Steve—the very one to whom Mr. Frog had just shown his sign.

"Pay up, please!" Ferdinand Frog said.

"How much do I owe you?" the uneasy Beaver asked him.

"Sixty!" Mr. Frog told him, with a grin.

Stingy Steve thrust his hand inside the pocket of his new trousers, from which he slowly drew one of Mr. Frog's tape-measures—of which the tailor had at least a dozen. Mr. Frog was always tucking them away in odd places.

"Here!" Stingy Steve cried. "Here's your pay—sixty inches, neither more nor less!"

But Ferdinand Frog only laughed and told him that he didn't mean inches. That, he explained, was no pay at all.

"I know," Stingy Steve replied. "I know it's not the fashionable way to pay a bill at present. But it will be five years from now. And what's more, you can't prove that what I say isn't true."

For a few moments Mr. Frog stood there gasping. And pretty soon he noticed that his customers were all busily picking up chips and sticks and pebbles. At first he thought they were going to throw them at him; and he was all ready to jump.

But he soon found that he was mistaken.

"Here! Here's your pay, Mr. Frog!" they began to cry. And to their astonishment Mr. Frog began to laugh.

"I don't want any pay," he declared. "Will you all promise to wear your new clothes if I make them free?"

"Yes! Yes! Yes!" sounded on all sides.

"Then it's a bargain!" Ferdinand Frog shouted. And he leaped into the air and kicked his heels together three times.

After that he turned a back somersault, and then he rolled over and over until he landed with a great splash in the pond.

Deep down on the muddy bottom Mr. Frog laughed as if he could never stop. The Beavers on the bank could neither see nor hear him. And he knew there was no danger of their thinking him impolite, especially when he said:

"They don't even know that I've played a trick on them! And what a terrible sight they are! I've never seen any company that looked the least bit like them."

XVI

STOP THAT!

On a cool summer's morning Ferdinand Frog was sitting among the reeds near the bank of the pond when a harsh voice suddenly said:

"Stop that!"

Looking up, Mr. Frog saw a huge bird standing on one leg in the water, watching him. The stranger was actually so big that Mr. Frog hadn't noticed him.

To be sure, he had seen what he thought was a stick stuck upright in the muddy bottom of the pond. That was really the stranger's leg; but Mr. Frog hadn't taken the trouble to glance upwards and see what was at the top of it.

Of course, Mr. Frog was frightened as soon as he discovered his mistake, for the bird had a great, long bill. Without being told, Ferdinand Frog knew that that bill could open like a trap—and seize him, too. But he showed not the least sign that he was even disturbed.

"Stop that, I say!" the stranger repeated, before Mr. Frog had so much as said a word.

"Stop what?" Mr. Frog asked.

"Stop sticking your tongue out at me!" the other commanded.

In spite of his alarm, when he heard that Ferdinand Frog began to laugh.

"I beg your pardon," he said, "but I think you are mistaken. I wasn't sticking my tongue out at you. I was only catching flies." Mr. Frog paid no attention to the sneering laugh that the stranger gave. "You see," he went on, "I'm having my breakfast. And this is how I manage it: I wait here without moving until a fly comes my way. Then I dart my tongue at him as quick as lightning.

"My tongue," Mr. Frog explained, "is fastened at the front of my mouth instead of at the back. So I can often reach a fly when he thinks he's perfectly safe. And furthermore, my tongue is so sticky that if it touches a fly, he can't get away. Then I swallow that one and wait for another."

"A likely story!" the big bird scoffed. "I've been watching you for a long time (Mr. Frog shivered when he heard that!) and I know what I'm talking about. . . . There you go again!" he shrieked angrily, as Ferdinand Frog's tongue flew out and captured another fly so quickly that the stranger couldn't see just what had happened.

"Listen to me a moment!" Mr. Frog said. "Like most people, I have to eat. And when I eat I can't help sticking out my tongue. So I'd suggest that if you don't care to watch me at my breakfast you'd better go away. It certainly isn't my fault that you're standing right in front of me."

But the stranger declined to move.

"If you really meant to be polite," he grumbled, "you'd at least turn your back when you stick out your tongue."

But Mr. Frog never stirred. He was afraid that the moment he turned his back the big bird would pounce upon him.

"It's not necessary for me to turn around now," he explained. "I've finished my breakfast. And I hope you've had yours, too."

"I'm sorry to say that I have," the stranger answered with a sigh, as he looked longingly at plump Mr. Frog. "I couldn't eat another mouthful if it sat right in front of me."

And then Ferdinand Frog felt as if a great weight had been lifted from his mind. He smiled all over his face, to show the stranger that he was glad to see him.

"Ah!" Mr. Frog cried. "Then we can have a friendly chat together. I always like to talk with travellers. . . . What a long, sharp bill you have!"

Now, some people would think that a rude remark. But it seemed to please the stranger immensely.

XVII

A LONG, SHARP BILL

Certainly it was an odd remark that Ferdinand Frog made about the stranger's wicked-looking bill. But knowing that its owner had eaten until he had no appetite left for the time being, Mr. Frog forgot his fear. And he couldn't help being curious about the big bird, because he had never seen another like him.

Of course, what Mr. Frog said would have annoyed some people a good deal, for he had just the same as told the stranger that he had a long, sharp nose. But luckily it happened that the newcomer was very vain both of the length and the sharpness of his bill. So he liked Mr. Frog's comment. And he promptly forgot his displeasure over Mr. Frog's tongue.

"Yes!" he said, in response to Ferdinand Frog's speech, "there isn't another bill like mine for twenty miles around—except my wife's."

"You don't live in this neighborhood, do you?" Mr. Frog inquired.

"My home is beyond the Second Mountain," the stranger informed him.

And Ferdinand Frog was glad to hear that the huge fellow dwelt no nearer.

"What's your name, friend?" Mr. Frog then asked.

"My name——" the giant bird replied—"my name is G. B. Heron."

"'G. B.'!" Mr. Frog exclaimed, turning a pale green color. "What do those letters stand for? Not Grizzly Bear, I hope!" He had heard of—but had never seen—a Grizzly Bear; and for a moment he thought that perhaps he had met one at last.

But the stranger soon set his fresh fears at rest.

"My full name," he told Mr. Frog, "is Great Blue Heron. But plain Mr. Heron will do, when you address me."

"I hope I'll see you sooner the next time we meet," Mr. Frog said. And he resolved that he would keep a sharp eye out for Mr. Heron, so that he might have plenty of time to hide the moment he caught sight of him.

"There's no doubt that we'll meet again," Mr. Heron replied. "I expect to come here to live. And I flew over here to-day to look about a bit. . . . Are there many in your family?"

"No!" Mr. Frog hastened to answer. "There's only myself living in this pond."

"But you must have plenty of relations somewhere," Mr. G. B. Heron insisted. "If I came here to live, and anything happened to you, I'd want to tell your family."

"Well, I have a few relations, to be sure," Mr. Frog admitted. "But they don't amount to much. They're a stringy lot, I can tell you."

Mr. Heron looked at him as if he couldn't quite believe that statement.

"That's odd," he observed. "Now, you're nice and plump."

"Oh, I'm too fat," Ferdinand Frog said. "Aunt Polly Woodchuck tells me that if I get much fatter I'll lose my good looks."

"I don't agree with her," said Mr. Heron. "You look good to me."

And now it was Mr. Frog's turn to be pleased; for he was very vain.

"I'm glad to hear it!" he cried. "And I'll tell you a secret: I've always been quite satisfied with myself until my eyes fell on you. Oh! if I only had such a bill as yours!"

"You like my bill, then?" Mr. Heron asked him.

"Yes!" Ferdinand Frog answered. "And it must be very handy, too."

"What for?" Mr. Heron inquired.

"Why, for making button-holes!" Ferdinand Frog exclaimed.

XVIII

MAKING BUTTON-HOLES

Mr. Heron couldn't help being interested.

"Button-holes in what?" he asked Ferdinand Frog.

"Why, in suits of clothes, of course!" the tailor answered. "If you had a tailor's shop, as I have, you'd find that bill of yours a handy thing to have. When you wanted to make a button-hole in a piece of cloth all you'd need do would be to stick your bill through it."

"I'd like to try that," Mr. Heron remarked.

"Then come right over to my shop," Mr. Frog urged him. "I'll let you make all the button-holes you want."

"Very well!" Mr. Heron agreed. "I'll make button-holes until I get hungry."

"That's a good idea!" Mr. Frog cried. And his new friend smiled, for he thought the tailor must be very stupid. He intended to stay with Mr. Frog until he was hungry enough to eat him. And no one who wasn't dull-witted could have failed to grasp his plan.

Well, they started off together; and they arrived shortly afterward at the tailor's shop.

Observing that Mr. Heron was altogether too big to squeeze inside the tiny building, Mr. Frog entered it, to reappear soon with an armful of cloth.

On this Mr. Frog proceeded to mark a row of dots. And then he hung the cloth upon some reeds.

"There!" he announced. "Can you hit the mark?"

"Certainly I can," Mr. Heron replied. And quick as lightning his sharp bill darted out and made a neat hole exactly where every dot had been.

"Splendid! Perfect!" Mr. Frog exclaimed. And thereupon he brought forth more cloth.

In a surprisingly short time Mr. Heron had made eighty-seven button-holes. But Mr. Frog noticed that beginning with the seventy-seventh button-hole the stranger's aim began to fail. He did not hit the dots quite squarely. And he seemed not to have his mind on his work.

"What's the matter?" Mr. Frog inquired. "Are you getting tired?"

"No—not tired," Mr. Heron told him.

"Are your eyes troubling you?" the tailor asked him.

"No—I can see well enough," Mr. Heron replied. "But I'm beginning to feel a bit faint. And I think I've made enough button-holes for one day."

But Mr. Frog said that he had a special suit which he was making for somebody. And he begged Mr. Heron to make the button-holes in that too.

Mr. Heron frowned. But presently he yielded, telling Mr. Frog to hurry, for he had another matter to attend to.

So the tailor leaped into his shop once more. And for a few moments he was very busy, arranging another strip of cloth so that the stranger might make button-holes in it.

When all was ready Mr. Heron stepped up to do his work. He was just about to strike, when he suddenly paused.

"Who's going to have this suit?" he asked the tailor.

"Mr. Fish Hawk," said the tailor. "Do you know him?"

"I should say I did!" Mr. Heron cried. "And he's no friend of mine, I assure you. I only wish he was behind this cloth! I'd run my bill clean through him!"

A cold, cruel glitter came into Mr. Heron's eyes. And when he struck, he struck with all his power, as if he were driving his wicked bill through Mr. Fish Hawk that very moment.

He made only that one thrust. And he did not withdraw his bill, either. Instead he set up a terrible squawking and began to flounder about on the bank of the pond.

"Help! Help!" he cried in a muffled voice.

But Ferdinand Frog only smiled—and made no move to assist his new acquaintance. The truth of the matter was that he had hidden a block of wood behind the cloth, and Mr. Heron had driven his bill into it so far that he couldn't pull it out.

With a loud chuckle Mr. Frog jumped into the water and swam away. And that very day he moved to Black Creek, without troubling himself to learn how Mr. Heron got himself out of his difficulty.

But the tailor couldn't help thinking what a handy thing it would be to have a bill like Mr. Heron's.

"He can even make button-holes in wood!" Mr. Frog exclaimed.

XIX

THE SWIMMING TEACHER

It surprised the wild folk in Pleasant Valley when they learned that Mr. Frog had forsaken the Beaver pond for a new home on the bank of Black Creek.

When his friends asked him why he had moved Mr. Frog told them he had made up his mind that the pond was too damp for the good of his health. Besides, Black Creek was nearer Cedar Swamp, where the Frog family held their singing-parties.

Of course, the real reason for Ferdinand Frog's change of scene was that he was afraid Mr. Heron might return to the Beaver pond some day, to look for him.

And when that happened, Mr. Frog did not care to be there.

In his new home, however, he felt quite at his ease. And he set out at once to make himself agreeable to his neighbors.

The nearest of these were Long Bill Wren and his wife, who at that time chanced to have a family of five growing children.

Mr. Frog took a great interest in the youngsters, who were already big enough to leave their ball-shaped home, which hung among the reeds, and hop about on the bank of the creek—and even fly a bit now and then.

Quite often Mr. Frog stopped to look at Long Bill's children and tell their parents how handsome they were.

"I suppose—" he said to their father one day——"I suppose you are going to teach them to swim?"

Long Bill Wren hadn't thought of that. And he said quickly that he was afraid it wouldn't be safe.

But Mr. Frog replied that it certainly wouldn't be safe not to, living as they did so close to the water.

"They're liable to tumble in almost any day," he said. "I suppose you can swim, yourself?"

"No!" Long Bill answered, looking somewhat worried. "I've never learned how."

Mr. Frog appeared greatly surprised by his neighbor's reply.

"Then I'd be glad to teach your children," he offered.

"Swimming is a very simple matter. And when you're young is the time to learn. I began when I was a tadpole. And knowing how to swim has saved my life a good many times."

Naturally the children were eager to have a lesson at once. And Long Bill Wren was about to yield to their teasing, when his wife happened to come flying home.

"What's going on here?" she asked sharply, for she saw that something unusual was afoot.

And when her husband explained Mr. Frog had kindly offered to teach the children to swim she cried, "The idea! I won't have it!"

Long Bill Wren looked uncomfortable. He was afraid his wife had hurt Mr. Frog's feelings.

But Mr. Frog smiled and bowed politely to Mrs. Wren.

"Surely you're not afraid your children will drown in my care?" he cried.

"No!" she told him. "The trouble is I'd be nervous, because one of my young brothers was eaten by a member of your family."

Ferdinand Frog's face fell. But not for long.

"I don't see how that could have come about," he declared. "It must have been an accident."

"Perhaps!" Long Bill's wife replied. "Anyhow, I want no such accidents to happen to my children." And she looked sternly at her new neighbor.

Mr. Frog glanced away uneasily.

"I'm afraid," he observed, "you do not trust me. But I assure you I had no idea of eating any of your little ones. They'd be perfectly safe with me. Why, every one of them is so plump I'd never be able to decide which one to choose first!"

He often wondered, afterward, why Mrs. Wren promptly called all her children into the house.

XX
DISTURBING THE NEIGHBORS

It was no wonder that Long Bill Wren's wife did not care for Ferdinand Frog, after his blundering remark about her children.

Though her husband often told her that Mr. Frog must have been merely joking, she insisted that he was not a safe person to have in the neighborhood.

"That Mr. Frog certainly is a queer one," she said to her husband one day. "I was watching him this morning. And what do you suppose I saw him do?" Mrs. Wren did not wait for Long Bill to answer her question. "Mr. Frog actually pulled off his own skin!" she cackled nervously.

"Cat-tails and pussy-willows!" Long Bill Wren exclaimed — which was his way of showing he was surprised. "Mr. Frog must be ill. Maybe I ought to go and tell Aunt Polly Woodchuck, the herb-doctor, and ask her to come over here at once."

His wife, however, shook her head.

"He can't be ill," she said.

"Why not?"

"His appetite is still good," she explained. "I saw Mr. Frog swallow his skin after he had pulled it off. And it didn't seem to disagree with him. He went in swimming right afterwards."

"Ah!" Long Bill exclaimed. "That's a very dangerous thing to do. At least, I've often heard Johnnie Green say that a boy ought not to go in the water sooner than a full hour after he has had a meal."

"There he is now!" Mrs. Wren cried abruptly. "There's Mr. Frog!"

Peeping out of the doorway on one side of his ball-shaped house, Long Bill could see Ferdinand Frog paddling about in Black Creek.

While they were watching him, he sank before their eyes. And after a time they couldn't help feeling uneasy, because their odd neighbor did not show himself again.

"I'm afraid——" Long Bill whispered at last——"I'm afraid he was taken with a cramp, for that's what you get by swimming too soon after a meal—so Johnnie Green says. . . . I'm glad now that we didn't let Mr. Frog teach our children to swim, because it's easy to see that he's a careless fellow."

So worried were Long Bill and his wife over Mr. Frog's disappearance that they hurried out and told all their neighbors about it. And soon a crowd had gathered upon the bank of the creek, to watch the spot where Mr. Frog had vanished.

They stayed there for a long time. But to their great alarm, their missing friend did not reappear.

"I hope he's safe," old Mr. Turtle piped in his thin, quavering voice. "He's making a new suit for me; and I'd hate to have anything happen to him."

"What's this—a party?" a voice called suddenly from under the bank. And then Mr. Frog himself, looking fine and fit, hopped up and stood before the company, with a broad grin on his face.

"Where have you been?" they shouted. "We were worried about you."

"Oh, I've been having a mud bath at the bottom of the creek," Mr. Frog told them. "Mud baths, you know, are very healthful. And I advise you all to try one."

XXI

MUD BATHS

Though Mr. Frog agreed cheerfully to show his neighbors how to take a mud bath, there wasn't even one of them that accepted his offer.

To be sure, old Mr. Turtle remarked that there was a good deal to be said about mud baths. And then he waddled to the water's edge and swam away.

"You heard what he said," Mr. Frog continued, turning to those who were left. "It's simple enough. All one has to do is to dive down to the bottom of the creek and bury himself snugly in the soft mud."

"How do you breathe?" somebody inquired.

"Oh, that's simple enough," Mr. Frog replied. "You breathe through your skin."

Smiles appeared on the faces of his listeners. And here and there a cough sounded. It was plain that the company had little faith in Mr. Frog's easy explanation.

"Doesn't it hurt your skin to breathe through it?" some one else asked.

"What if it does?" Ferdinand Frog retorted. "When your skin becomes worn, pull it off!"

Everybody laughed heartily at his answer; or at least, everybody except Long Bill Wren and his wife. They exchanged a thoughtful look. For they knew Mr. Frog's ways better than his other neighbors did.

Now, Ferdinand Frog did not mind the laughter at all.

"Of course," he went on, "you can't breathe through your skin quite so well as you can in the regular way. After you have stayed in the mud a while, you'll begin to want a regular breath of fresh air. So then you come up to the top of the water."

"Cat-tails and pussy-willows!" Long Bill Wren cried out. "I'm sure I shall never take a mud bath. They seem to me to be very dangerous."

"Not at all!" Mr. Frog assured him. "They're as safe as standing on your head." And thereupon he stood on his own head, to prove that what he said was true.

Still the company was not moved to take Mr. Frog's advice and try a mud bath. Most of them declared that nothing could induce them to undertake such a risky act. But a few daring ones said that if all the rest would take mud baths, and if they found that they liked them, they themselves would be willing to test them too.

However, nobody took a single step towards the creek. So at last the company scattered, leaving Long Bill Wren and Mr. Frog alone upon the bank.

Meanwhile Long Bill had been thinking deeply. He had begun to wonder whether there might not be some good in a mud bath, in spite of his neighbors' doubts. And now he turned to Ferdinand Frog and began speaking in a hushed voice.

"Don't tell my wife I asked you this question," he said; "but I should like to know if mud baths are good for rheumatism."

"Good for it!" Mr. Frog exclaimed. "Why, they're a sure cure—and the only one!"

XXII

LEARNING TO HOLD HIS BREATH

There on the bank of Black Creek Mr. Frog and Long Bill Wren talked in whispers about mud baths. And in a short time Long Bill announced that he had made up his mind to try one.

"Good!" Mr. Frog cried, as he patted his neighbor on the back. "And now let me give you a bit of advice. Before you dive into the creek you should learn to hold your breath. . . .

"You'd better go home and begin practising at once."

So Long Bill Wren flew into his house and stayed there the rest of that day. But he soon found that all was not as simple as he had hoped. Whenever he was trying to hold his breath his wife was sure to ask him a question. And of course that led to trouble. If he didn't answer her she thought him rude—and said so, quite frankly, too. While if he did answer her, speaking spoiled his practice.

It was annoying, to say the least. And by the next morning the poor fellow was almost frantic.

He sought out Mr. Frog and explained how hard it was for him to learn to hold his breath.

"If you could only think of some way of making my wife hold hers too!" Long Bill moaned.

But Mr. Frog said at once that nobody could do that, and there was no use in trying.

"Why don't you," he asked, "go off by yourself in Cedar Swamp, and practice there?"

But Long Bill said that he ought not to stay away from home long enough to do that.

"Then there's only one way left for you," Mr. Frog decided. "You must practice at night, when your wife's asleep."

"A good idea!" Long Bill whispered. "I'll try it this very night!"

Bright and early the next morning Long Bill Wren found Mr. Frog a little way up the creek and told him that his night's practice had been a great success.

"I began holding my breath right after sunset," he said, "and it was so easy that I fell asleep. And I never breathed once all night long, until I awoke at day-break."

The news delighted Mr. Frog.

"Good!" he cried. "And now there's one more thing you must do before you take a mud bath. You must learn to breathe through your skin. . . . Just try right now," he urged his companion.

So Long Bill tried to breathe through his skin, while holding his breath at the same time.

And soon he began to sputter and choke.

"I'm afraid I can't do it," he faltered at last.

Mr. Frog looked somewhat glum—for a moment.

He pondered in silence. And at length he declared that without doubt there must be something wrong with Long Bill's skin!

"How long have you worn it?" he inquired.

"All my life!" Long Bill told him.

"That's it!" Mr. Frog exclaimed. "It's worn out. You'll have to pull it off and use a fresh one."

XXIII

MR. FROG RUNS AWAY

It may have been Mr. Frog's words that dismayed Long Bill Wren, or it may have been his manner—or perhaps both. Anyhow, Long Bill looked frightened.

"Where can I get a fresh skin if I pull off the one I'm wearing?" he wanted to know.

"Why, there's another skin just beneath your old one," Mr. Frog informed him glibly. "Just pull hard and you'll see that I know what I'm talking about."

But Long Bill was puzzled.

"I—I don't know where to begin," he stammered.

"Maybe you need help," Mr. Frog suggested.

And Long Bill agreed that he did need help—and a good deal of it, too.

"Well," Mr. Frog said with a giggle, "I'll get old Mr. Turtle to assist me. And between us we'll have your old skin off before you know it."

He began to bellow Mr. Turtle's name at the top of his lungs. And soon the old gentleman's black head popped out of the water. And presently Mr. Turtle waddled up the bank of Black Creek and listened to Ferdinand Frog's directions.

"You take hold of Long Bill's tail," Mr. Frog ordered him, while to the frightened owner of the tail he said cheerfully, "Anything Mr. Turtle takes hold of just has to come. He never lets go until it does."

Now, Long Bill Wren had suddenly made up his mind that he wouldn't take a mud bath, after all. He didn't like the prospect of having his skin pulled off. Suppose Mr. Frog should be mistaken about that second skin, which the tailor claimed lay underneath the old one?

Long Bill believed that with no skin at all he would find his rheumatism much worse than before. And he would certainly be a queer-looking object.

So as old Mr. Turtle crawled slowly towards him, he drew away.

"I'm going to wait— —" Long Bill announced.

"Why?" Mr. Frog demanded.

"Going to wait till the weather is warmer," Long Bill faltered.

Of course Mr. Frog was disappointed by having his plans so upset.

And Mr. Turtle was disappointed too.

"My mouth is open," he told Mr. Frog. "I must grab something. And it might as well be you."

But Mr. Frog jumped nimbly out of Mr. Turtle's reach. And a moment later he thrust the free end of a tree-root between Mr. Turtle's jaws.

They closed with a snap. And Mr. Turtle began to pull.

"Come on!" Mr. Frog urged Long Bill Wren. "The tree may fall at any moment. It's safer elsewhere." And without waiting to see what happened, he leaped into Black Creek and swam away.

As for Long Bill Wren, he hurried home. He knew his wife would be wondering where he was, for he had been away from the house in the reeds much longer than his usual ten minutes.

Arriving there, he was not surprised that she asked him a few questions. And he explained to her that he had been on the bank of the creek, watching old Mr. Turtle pulling at the root of a willow.

"And I can tell you that I'm well pleased that it wasn't my tail Mr. Turtle had in his jaws," he said solemnly.

Mrs. Wren shuddered at the mere mention of such an unlucky accident. And then she said: "I hope that dangerous Mr. Frog was not with you."

"I believe he was there for a time," her husband replied. "But he left before I did."

"I wish you would keep away from him," she remarked.

"I'm going to," Long Bill Wren promised. "Although Mr. Frog is our newest neighbor, I shall have nothing more to do with him."

THE END